Fantastic Frogs

Written by Carol Krueger

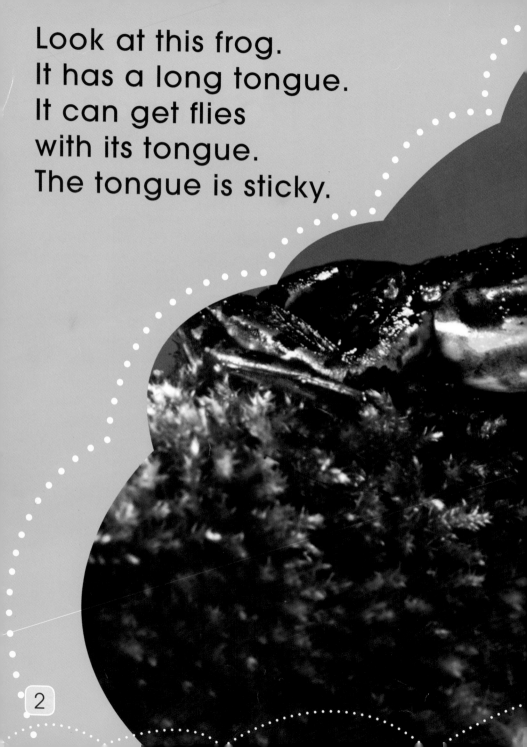

Look at this frog.
It has a long tongue.
It can get flies
with its tongue.
The tongue is sticky.

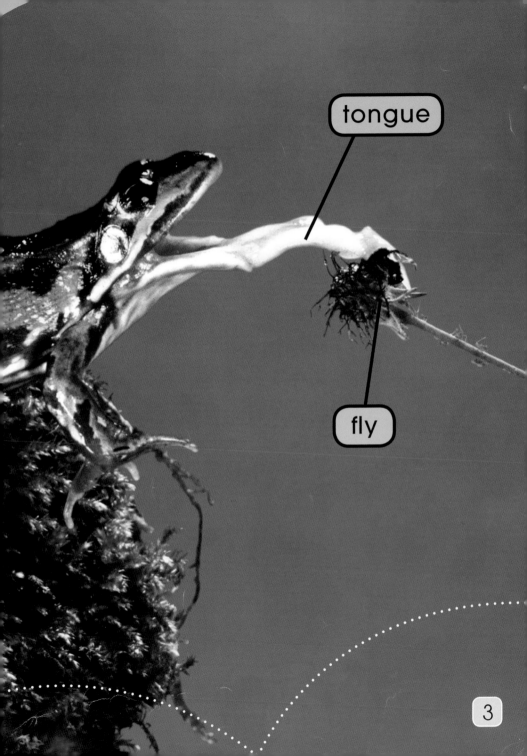

tongue

fly

3

This frog has fingers and toes.
They are sticky, too.

It can climb up
leaves and grass!

toes

fingers

5

Look at the legs on this frog.
It has long legs.
The frog can jump out
of the water.
It can jump away fast, too.

This frog is jumping
from the tree.
It can jump in the air.
When it jumps,
it can get insects.

This frog takes care of
its babies.
The babies are
in its mouth.
When the babies grow,
they will hop out.

tadpole

mouth

This frog is small.
It can sit on a fingernail.
But this little frog can eat
a lot of insects.

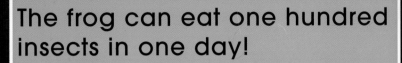
The frog can eat one hundred insects in one day!

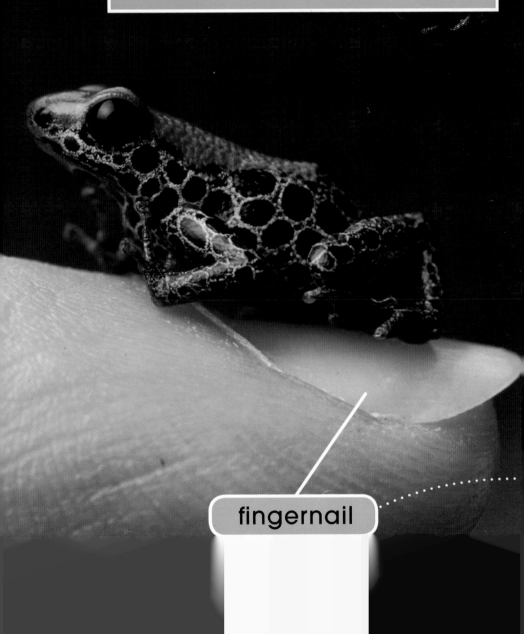
fingernail

Frogs can help people.
Some insects eat plants
in the garden.
Frogs eat the insects.

garden

Index

▬▬▬ Guide Notes

Title: Fantastic Frogs
Stage: Early (3) – Blue

Genre: Nonfiction
Approach: Guided Reading
Processes: Thinking Critically, Exploring Language, Processing Information
Written and Visual Focus: Photographs (static images), Index, Labels, Caption
Word Count: 138

THINKING CRITICALLY
(sample questions)
- Look at the front cover and the title. Ask the children what they know about frogs.
- Look at the title and read it to the children.
- Focus the children's attention on the index. Ask: "What are you going to find out about in this book?"
- If you want to find out about a frog that can climb, which page would you look on?
- If you want to find out about a frog with a sticky tongue, which page would you look on?
- Look at pages 6 and 7. What do you think the frog could be jumping away from?
- Look at pages 10 and 11. Why do you think the frog keeps its babies in its mouth?

EXPLORING LANGUAGE

Terminology
Title, cover, photographs, author, photographers

Vocabulary
Interest words: frog, sticky, flies, fingers, toes, tongue, leaves, insects, fingernail
High-frequency words: fast, lot, eat, from, when
Positional words: up, out, in, on
Compound word: fingernail

Print Conventions
Capital letter for sentence beginnings, periods, commas, exclamation mark